W9-AGZ-674
LG
BL: 2.7
AR: 0.5

Fuchsia FIERCE

Written by

CHRISTIANNE JONES

Illustrated by

KELLY CANBY

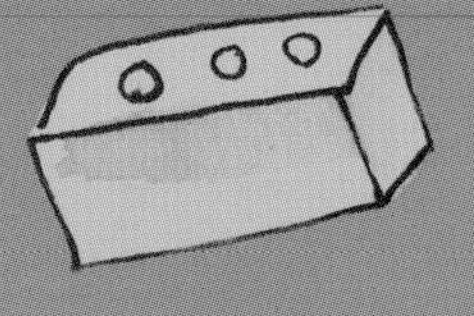

Picture Window Books
a capstone imprint

FUCHSIA FIERCE

was a bold name for a little girl.

But Fuchsia wasn't

BOLD OR **FIERCE**.

She was quiet, shy, tiny, and timid.

She was scared to try new things
or stand out in a crowd.

ICE CREAM

So Fuchsia's parents decided to help her.
You're sending me away?

"I know you're scared," her mom said. "But you will love **CAMP CONFIDENCE**."

"Okay," Fuchsia said, but her stomach hurt just thinking about it.

Upon arrival, Fuchsia quickly decided she wasn't going to let Camp Confidence change her. She would do what she always did –

MAKE UP EXCUSES

so she didn't have to try anything new.

welcome
CAMP
CONFIDENCE

For a while, it worked.
Fuchsia, it's time for swimming.
I forgot my swimsuit.
Then you can sit on the dock and watch your friends.

Fuchsia, it's time to try the climbing wall.
I can't. I hurt my finger.
Then you can help with the equipment.

Fuchsia,
it's your turn to
tell a ghost story.

I can't.
I lost my voice.

Then you can
write a story and
I will read it.

By the end of the week, Fuchsia was running out of excuses and getting bored. Everyone else was having

SO MUCH FUN.

By the end of the week, Fuchsia was running out of excuses and getting bored. Everyone else was having

SO MUCH FUN.

On game night, Fuchsia saw the
perfect chance to end her boredom.

When her turn rolled around,
everyone was ready for
another excuse.

But that excuse never came.
Instead, Fuchsia took a deep breath ...

. . . AND WALKED
TO THE FRONT
OF THE ROOM!

Fuchsia was nervous, but nobody laughed.
They shouted out answers and cheered.
It wasn't embarrassing — it was awesome!

After that, Fuchsia started to try new things —

even if they were hard or scary.

Was she the best at
everything she tried?

NOPE.

But that was okay.

With every activity,
Fuchsia's confidence grew.

"I will be a
SUPERHERO PRINCESS!"
S

She even learned that being tiny
wasn't such a bad trait.

And when Fuchsia called home,
she had a lot to say.

"I love horseback riding
and soccer, but not tennis.

I'm trying to learn to play
guitar, but it is really hard.

Turns out I'm good at building things.

I still can't do a cartwheel,
but I'm going to keep trying.

And most of all,
I'm having fun!"

At times, Fuchsia still felt
quiet, shy, tiny, and timid.

But she learned to be brave and strong and fearless, too. She learned to **BELIEVE IN HERSELF.**

1
2
3
1
2
3

She learned that Fuchsia Fierce
really could be

FIERCE.

3

To Lalayna, Lola, and Hattie.
Be bold. Be fierce. Be fearless. Be happy. –C.J.

To Angie, Elizabeth, Annabel, Amelia, Ashleigh, and Tess.
Move mountains. –K.C.

Fuchsia Fierce is published by
Picture Window Books, a Capstone imprint
1710 Roe Crest Drive, North Mankato, Minnesota 56003
www.mycapstone.com

Library of Congress Cataloging-in-Publication Data
is available on the Library of Congress website.

ISBN: 978-1-62370-786-6 (paper-over-board)
ISBN: 978-1-5158-0553-3 (library binding)
ISBN: 978-1-5158-0554-0 (eBook pdf)

Designer: Aruna Rangarajan
Creative Director: Heather Kindseth Wutschke

Printed in the United States of America.
092016 010070R